**Dear Parents,**

Welcome to the Scholastic Reader series. We have taken over 80 years of experience with teachers, parents, and children and put it into a program that is designed to match your child's interests and skills.

**Level 1**—Short sentences and stories made up of words kids can sound out using their phonics skills and words that are important to remember.

**Level 2**—Longer sentences and stories with words kids need to know and new "big" words that they will want to know.

**Level 3**—From sentences to paragraphs to longer stories, these books have large "chunks" of texts and are made up of a rich vocabulary.

**Level 4**—First chapter books with more words and fewer pictures.

It is important that children learn to read well enough to succeed in school and beyond. Here are ideas for reading this book with your child:

- Look at the book together. Encourage your child to read the title and make a prediction about the story.
- Read the book together. Encourage your child to sound out words when appropriate. When your child struggles, you can help by providing the word.
- Encourage your child to retell the story. This is a great way to check for comprehension.
- Have your child take the fluency test on the last page to check progress.

Scholastic Readers are designed to support your child's efforts to learn how to read at every age and every stage. Enjoy helping your child learn to read and love to read.

　　　　—**Francie Alexander**
　　　　　Chief Education Officer
　　　　　Scholastic Education

For my friend Jessie
–C.D.


For B.F.–
Who in his travels has occasionally
fallen into the muck.
–L.R.

Library of Congress Cataloging-in-Publication Data available

ISBN: 0-439-79431-5

10 9 8 7 6 5 4          06 07 08 09 10 11

Printed in the U.S.A. 23 • First printing, April 2006

# YUCK!
## STUCK IN THE MUCK

by Corinne Demas
Illustrated by Laura Rader

**Scholastic Reader — Level 1**

Cartwheel
·B·O·O·K·S·®

SCHOLASTIC INC.

New York  Toronto  London  Auckland  Sydney
Mexico City  New Delhi  Hong Kong  Buenos Aires

Dog chased Duck
into the swamp.

Duck flew up.
Dog got stuck in the muck.

Chuck jumped into the
swamp to pull out Dog.

Chuck got stuck
in the muck.

Donkey came to pull Dog
and Chuck from the swamp.

Donkey got stuck
in the muck.

Sue set out in a boat to pull
Donkey and Dog and Chuck
from the swamp.

Sue's boat got stuck in the muck.

Sam set out in a truck
to pull Sue's boat and
Donkey and Dog and Chuck
from the swamp.

Sam's truck
got stuck
in the muck.

A helicopter came to pluck
Sam and Sue and Chuck
and Donkey and Dog
from the muck.

First it plucked out Dog.

# Then Donkey.

# Then Sue.

# Then Sam.

They each took
a bath to wash
off all the guck.

Duck flew back to
the swamp and found
the truck.

# Fluency Fun

The words in each list below end in the same sounds.
Read the words in a list.
Read them again.
Read them faster.
Try to read all 12 words in one minute.

| | | |
|---|---|---|
| **duck** | **boat** | **came** |
| **yuck** | **coat** | **game** |
| **stuck** | **goat** | **name** |
| **truck** | **float** | **same** |

Look for these words in the story.

| | | |
|---|---|---|
| **her** | **pull** | **from** |
| | **off** | **out** |

**Note to Parents:**

According to *A Dictionary of Reading and Related Terms*, fluency is "the ability to read smoothly, easily, and readily with freedom from word-recognition problems." Fluency is necessary for good comprehension and enjoyable reading. The activities on this page include a speed drill and a sight-recognition drill. Speed drills build fluency because they help students rapidly recognize common syllables and spelling patterns in words, and they're fun! Sight-recognition drills help students smoothly and accurately recognize words. Practice these activities with your child to help him or her become a fluent reader.

—**Wiley Blevins**,
Reading Specialist